BEAN DOG
and
NUGGET

The Ball

Charise Mericle Harper

ed A. Knopf

Knopf, Borzoi Books, and the colophon are registered trademarks of Random House, Inc.

Visit us on the Web! randomhouse.com/kids

Educators and librarians, for a variety of teaching tools, visit us at RHTeachersLibrarians.com

Library of Congress Cataloging-in-Publication Data

Harper, Charise Mericle.

Bean Dog and Nugget : the ball / Charise Mericle Harper. — 1st ed.

 p. cm.— (Bean Dog and Nugget)

Summary: Bean Dog and Nugget lose Bean Dog's shiny new ball in a bush.
They dream up elaborate and silly ways to get it back while they argue
about who is actually going to go and get it.

ISBN 978-0-307-97707-6 (pbk.) — ISBN 978-0-307-97708-3 (lib. bdg.) — ISBN 978-0-307-97709-0 (ebook)

1. Graphic novels. [1. Graphic novels. 2. Lost and found possessions—Fiction.
3. Friendship—Fiction. 4. Humorous stories.] I. Title.

PZ7.7.H37Beb 2013

741.5 973—dc23

2012029373

The text of this book is set in 16-point Matt Md Text.
The illustrations were created using digital coloring.

MANUFACTURED IN MALAYSIA

May 2013   10 9 8 7 6 5 4 3 2 1   First Edition

For Luther and Cole,
two great boys

Wait, we don't have any of those things.

You're right.

That's too bad. I was really hoping for monkeys.

Ready for a snack, it's . . .